MiSTER iNViNCiBLE

WRITTEN AND ILLUSTRATED BY
PASCAL JOUSSELIN

COLORED BY
LAURENCE CROIX

Translation by David Bryon, James Hogan, and Ivanka T. Hahnenberger
Layout, Localization, and Editing by Mike Kennedy

6|21 ISBN: 978-1-942367-61-1

Library of Congress Control Number: 2020903057

Second Printing. Printed in China.

10 9 8 7 6 5 4 3 2

FOR MY PARENTS,
AND A BIG THANK-YOU TO
MATHILDE, FRED & LAURENCE.

- PASCAL

01

JOUSSELIN –
COLORS: CROIX

AHA! Here it is!

02

Jousselin -
colors: Croix

JOUSSELIN -
COLORS: CROIX

GUESS WHAT? IT'S...
MISTER INVINCIBLE
THE ONE AND ONLY TRUE COMIC BOOK SUPERHERO!

STOP, THIEF!!
?!

It's... it's MARATHON Mike... HUFF... the FAMOUS thief!
HUFF... No one's ever BEEN ABLE to CATCH HIM!

?!
MR. INVINCIBLE?
?!

HA! Gets me every time!
03
JOUSSELIN
COLORS: CROIX

HA HA HA! END OF THE LINE, MR. INVINCIBLE!

MY KILLER ROBOTS WILL CRUSH YOU, FOOLISH HERO!

05

COLORS: CROIX

07

JOUSSELIN —
COLORS: CROIX

10

JOUSSELIN —
COLORS: CROIX

Hello there, friends!
Hello, Mr. Mayor.
So, how's it looking?

Should take two or three days, sir. First we're gonna dig a trench to run the cables there, and then...
Very good, son, very good.
?! What?

Our bocce ball court! What are you doing to our bocce ball court?!

Ahh, good news, my friends! This square's about to enter the 21st century!

Take a look at this. Isn't it amazing?

Adtron 3000
Next-generation advertising
Ultra 3D effects!
8 hyper-definition screens!
Bring your ad to life!
Mega digital sound!
Adtron 3000: Embrace the future

What? You're going to destroy our court to install this mechanical thing?!
But, Mr. Mayor, you told us you'd never touch our bocce ball court!
You said that during your election campaign, remember?

I did...? Hmm... But things have changed! We need to embrace the future!

You promised. You're a liar.
Hey now...
Jack, buddy... Calm down! Deep breaths!
Ohhh... Why'd you have to lie to him? Now we're in for it!

KLANG
A man's gotta keep his word.

Wh... What happened to that sign?!
Oh no!
Take cover!

12-1

Did you see that? It suddenly got all bashed in...!

THAT...
...is the power...
...of words.

WHAT THE...?! It felt like A BUNCH OF invisible things attacked me...
It's the power of words, I said! You don't listen, MR. LIAR!
??!
?

ALL RIGHT NOW, THAT'S ENOUGH! I AM NOT A LIAR! IN FACT, I'VE NEVER LIED IN MY LIFE!
GRRRRR

MISTER INVINCIBLE
THE ONE AND ONLY TRUE COMIC BOOK SUPERHERO!
IN
THE WORDSMITH
RING-A-LING ♫

HELLO?
Mr. Invincible? Police Captain Jean-Pierre here.

We need your help, Mr. Invincible. It's a total mess out here!

All right. Don't move and keep talking.
HUH?! UH... OKAY, BUT YOU'd better come quick! It's getting dicey. We're in the main square...

WHAT's the problem?
Well, it's a bit hard to explain on the phone... you'll have to see it with your own eyes...

Hi.
AAAA

Geez... I... you... phew...!
WHAT HAPPENED HERE? AN EARTHQUAKE?

Wait, there's an elderly man over there! He could be in danger!
THAT's just it. Old Grandpa Jack is the one who did all this!
12-2

Ah, Mr. Invincible! Finally!
Hello, Mr. Mayor.
Stop that criminal immediately!

But watch out, he can do... strange things. It's as if... how can I explain...
You there! Why don't you show us? Go try to arrest him again!
HUH?!

But... er... um...
It's just that...
He's not gonna wanna see us...
JUST DO IT!

Er... sorry, Mr. Jack... but we have to ask you again to leave.
Eh?! Did the mayor agree not to dig up our Bocce ball court?
Ah... No, not exactly, sir...

In that case, I'm staying...
...protecting our court. Got it?

You see that? It's like there's some kind of invisible force at work here!
Incredible.

Same as before... He's says we should leave the Bocce ball court alone.
I will not negotiate with terrorists, do you hear me?! Never!

CAFÉ
Ooh, things are getting good! It's Mr. Invincible's turn!

Excuse me, sir... what's the deal with this Bocce ball court?

Pssst... young man...
?

SCRAM!

12-3

Oof... Let's try AGAIN.

I THINK WE MISUNDERSTAND EACH OTHER... I'd JUST LIKE TO HEAR YOUR SIDE OF THE STORY.

?!
No USE TRYING TO PULL A FAST ONE ON ME, SON. I KNOW WHOSE SIDE YOU'RE ON. I SAW YOU WITH YOUR FRIEND THE MAYOR.

I CAN'T STAND THAT MAN'S LIES.

LYING MEANS HAVING NO RESPECT FOR WORDS. AND THAT'S SOMETHING I CANNOT TOLERATE!

YOU SHOULDN'T UNDERESTIMATE THE POWER OF WORDS... WORDS CAN MOVE MOUNTAINS!

WHOA, MR. INVINCIBLE CAN FLY?

AH... NOPE.

NOW, YOU MAY THINK KEEPING QUIET IS DANGEROUS, TOO. AND YOU'D BE RIGHT...

OLD GRANDPA JACK'S PRETTY INCREDIBLE. I DIDN'T KNOW HE HAD SUPERPOWERS!
OH NO...
He's FINE MOST OF THE TIME. BUT WHEN YOU GET HIM MAD...

SO WHAT IS IT THE MAYOR WANTS TO PUT IN HERE, ANYWAY?
AN Ad 3000.

THIS THING?! RIGHT IN FRONT OF MY CAFE?!
WHAT, VIDEO ADS OUTSIDE MY WINDOW?
IS THIS A JOKE?

12-4

Well-chosen words can paralyze your enemies...
?!

Words can hurt!
BONK BONK BONK

And they can also lift you up, too...

?! WHAT THE... WHY'S He doing A HEAdstand?

Mastering language -- TRULY mastering it -- gives you incredible power...
His power comes from words...?

Almost, infinite power...
...NOTHING TO LOSE!

WHO THE HECK--?! YOU'RE GOING TO REGR--

HUSH! ENOUGH words!
M... M...

MM M MM
Please forgive me, but I'm going to have to confiscate your...

...dentures.
No intelligible words, no power of language!
'ir! Gimme 'y 'ee' 'ack!

Now, tell me what's going on.
What's all this uproar about?

I's 'im, 'e 'ayor. 'ir'y 'iar!
Ah, shoot... you can't talk. Maybe if you tried miming?

?! What are they...?
HEY! MR. MAYOR!
???

NO WAY YOU'RE PUTTING THIS MONSTROSITY IN THE MIDDLE OF THE SQUARE!
YEAH!
Are you crazy or what?

12-5

12-6

Jousselin

COLORS: CROIX

HE'S THE CURE FOR CRIME! HE'S

THE ONE AND ONLY TRUE COMIC BOOK SUPERHERO!

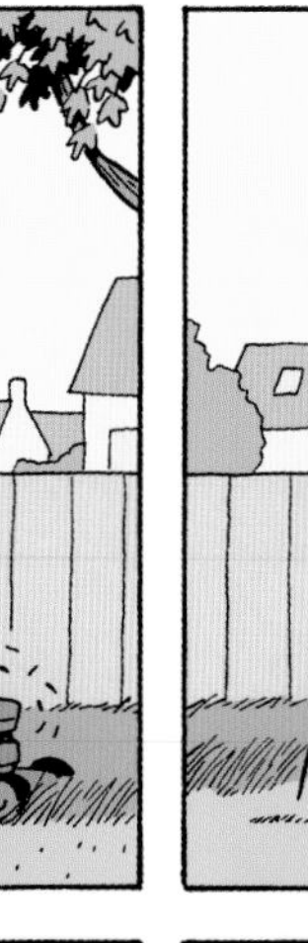

08

JOUSSELIN – COLORS: CROIX

IF HE DID MAGIC SHOWS, HE'D BE RICH.

14

Jousselin -
COLORS: CROIX

35

JOUSSELIN -
COLORS: CROIX.

MISTER INVINCIBLE
THE ONE AND ONLY TRUE COMIC BOOK SUPERHERO!
IN
THE DISAPPEARANCE OF Z!

AH, MR. INVINCIBLE! THERE YOU ARE!
?!
Of course. it's pot roast Sunday...
Oh, look, it's little Jean-Pierre!

Sit down, Jean-Pierre! Help yourself to some food!
Sorry, ma'am, no time! We need Mr. Invincible right away!

To fix that broken railroad crossing on Forest Avenue?
Huh?! No, no, we can take care of that on our own...
Well, it's been broken for three days now...

You should really get yourself a cell phone, Mr. Invincible! I've been trying to get hold of you for hours!

There's a lunatic on the roof of the community center asking to see you! We told him you'd come, but when you didn't show up he got mad and started breaking things!
?

Oh boy, I see... your van!
What? No, no, my van's fine right over there. Our cars, on the other hand...

WHY DON'T YOU TELL INVINCIBLE ABOUT ME, YOU BUNCH OF IDIOTS?!
Hmm. That's a strange voice.
Yeah, his megaphone sounds broken...

THAT'S ENOUGH!
Yikes! Here we go again!

WHY WON'T YOU LISTEN TO ME?!

WHY ARE YOU LYING TO ME?!
There... see?!
I've got this.
IT'S REALLY ANNOYING!

What's all this racket about?
?!

13-1

M-MR. INVINCIBLE?! IT'S REALLY YOU?!

AH... THE WEIRD VOICE IS BECAUSE YOU'RE A TEENAGER!
UM YEAH... MY UH... MY VOICE IS CHANGING. I CAN'T HELP IT.

WELL THEN. WHAT DO YOU WANT?
AHEM... HMM...

SUP! I'M 2-D BOY! X TO THE Y, Y'ALL!
99 PROBLEMS BUT A Z AIN'T ONE!

X TO THE... WHAT?!
UHH... IT'S MATH... AHEM... I MEAN, I'LL SHOW YOU...

OKAY! SHOW TIME...!
HMM... NO MORE CARS, SO...

?!

WHAT THE...?!
BOOM! 2-D POWER!

AND... LET ME HIT YOU AGAIN! YO, YO!
HEEY!
CREEEAK

YO, TWO-DEE BOY IS IN DA HOUSE!
ALRIGHT! STOP THAT RIGHT NOW OR I'LL ...

OR WHAT?! I DON'T WANNA FIGHT YOU, SIR!
YOU'RE MY IDOL!
HUH?

I WANTED TO MEET YOU BECAUSE MY HIGH SCHOOL TEACHER SAID WE HAVE TO DO AN INTERNSHIP... AND, WELL, I WANNA BE A SUPERHERO, SO...

YOU WANT TO BE A SUPERHERO BUT YOU'RE DESTROYING PUBLIC PROPERTY?!
ARE YOU OUT OF YOUR MIND, YOUNG MAN?! THINK FOR A SECOND!

WELL, ER... NO, YOU SEE... IT'S JUST... THE POLICE THOUGHT I WAS A BIG FAT LIAR. SO I... I JUST WANTED TO SHOW YOU MY SUPERPOWERS... SO THAT YOU'D WANNA TAKE ME ON AS YOUR INTERN...

LOOKS LIKE INVINCIBLE'S MANAGED TO REASON WITH THIS LOON.
LET'S GO!
19-2

Well? Are you coming?
Uhh... wouldn't it be better if we waited for a signal from Mr. Invincible, Chief?

Guys, it's our duty as police officers to maintain public order and safety... And we can't do that hiding behind trash cans! Let's show some backbone!
Come on!

FORWARD!

FALL BACK!

There you go...
CRREEAKK

Done. See? Everything's back to normal...
And the cars?

Ahem... yeah, uh... I can't fix that...
...sorry.

But to make up for it, I can help the police! I'll catch criminals, save lives... my superpowers could really come in handy!
Besides, I still have another week of vacation left.

Hmm.
OK.

He was right. Those superpowers are pretty useful!
Yeah, that Toodée is a good kid!

Next train in 37 minutes.
Pfffff
...so when does school start up again?

Jousselin -
COLORS: CROIX.

HE'S TAKING ON INTERNS...

JOUSSELIN —
COLORS: CROIX.

IN WINTER, GRAM-GRAM'S SCARF KEEPS HIM TOASTY!
MISTER INVINCIBLE
THE ONE AND ONLY TRUE COMIC BOOK SUPERHERO!

MR. MAYOR, THE CEO OF PESTICHEM HAS ARRIVED.
WELL, WHAT ARE YOU WAITING FOR? SEND HER IN!

MADAM CEO! IT'S AN HONOR TO RECEIVE THE DISTINGUISHED LEADER OF THE CITY'S MOST IMPORTANT COMPANY...
ALRIGHT.

I'LL BE BRIEF. I'M HERE BECAUSE WE'RE VERY INTERESTED IN ONE OF YOUR CITIZENS: MR. INVINCIBLE.
DO YOU KNOW HIM?

MR. INVINCIBLE? OF COURSE! HE'S A GOOD FRIEND!
WHAT WOULD YOU LIKE, MADAM CEO? AN AUTOGRAPH? PHOTO?

...
I HAVE NO PATIENCE FOR HUMOR, OR ANYTHING ELSE THAT WASTES MY PRECIOUS TIME.
I... HEH... UM...

I'D LIKE MR. INVINCIBLE TO BE ASSOCIATED WITH OUR PRODUCTS. HIS SUPERHERO STATUS PERFECTLY REPRESENTS THE SUPER STRENGTH OF OUR PESTICIDES.

WELL... IT'S... JUST... MR. INVINCIBLE ISN'T THE KIND OF GUY WHO...
I GET IT. YOU WANT A SLICE OF THE PIE. FINE.

HERE'S HOW MUCH WE'LL PAY YOU IF YOU CAN CONVINCE MR. INVINCIBLE TO ENDORSE OUR PRODUCT.
?

EEEEEEEEK...

GET MR. INVINCIBLE ON THE LINE, RIGHT AWAY!

THANKS! AND HAPPY HOLIDAYS!

MR. INVINCIBLE, MY FRIEND! HA HA HA! HOW'S IT GOING?
EH?! IT'S ME! YOUR OLD PAL, THE MAYOR!

HA HA. WHAT A JOKER!
LISTEN, BUDDY, I NEED TO SEE YOU. BUSINESS TO DISCUSS.

BUSINESS?! UH, MR. MAYOR, YOU KNOW I NEVER USE MY SUPERPOWERS FOR MONETARY GAIN...

30-1

JOUSSELIN —
COLORS: CROIX.

Mr. Invincible? It's Two-Dee boy. I'm in position on the edge of the forest...
...I can see you in your yard!
TROUBLE FOR TOODEE!
A MISTER INVINCIBLE ADVENTURE!

But... uhh... Are you sure you want to try this? I-I've never transported people before...

It's okay, Toodee, don't worry...

...it's the coat rack you'll be moving, not me!
Besides, you need to practice! Imagine if you have to save people from a burning building some day...
Uh... okay. I'll do it... just hold on...

That's it, Toodee!
But, uh... keep your arm straight. I'd like to stay my normal size...

Prepare to be vaporized, wretched city!

My annihilation ray is going to turn you into a gigantic black hole! Ha ha ha!
Mr. Invincible! I got a problem here...

Sorry? I can't hear you, Toodee...

A few more seconds and the ray will be charged heh heh heh!
There's a crazy guy with some kind of bazooka... he's gonna shoot it at the city! What do I do?!
What? Speak up, Toodee!
TIP TIP TIP

I can't or the crazy guy'll hear me!
?!
Hey, careful, Toodee! Watch out for that streetlight-BONK!

Mr. Invincible?!
Oh no! What have I done?!

31-1

RAY READY.
OH NO... THAT CRAZY DUDE...
HEH HEH HEH! HERE WE GO! 3... 2... 1...
SSS...

NOOOOO!
?!

??!
WHY WAS I TALKING ABOUT MOONBOOTS?!
FREEZE, YOU STUPID BRAT, OR I'LL OBLITERATE YOU!

YEAH, THAT'S RIGHT! FLEE WHILE YOU STILL CAN!

YOU CAN RUN, BUT YOU'LL BE ATOMIZED LIKE ALL THE OTHERS! HEE HEE HEE!

COME TO THINK OF IT, THAT SHOT FROM EARLIER SHOULD HAVE DONE SOME DAMAGE...
?

PERFECT! NOW IT'S
TO FINISH OFF THIS

HUFFF...
HFF...
THIS SHOULD WORK...

AAAAAH

YES!

W-WH... WHAT WAS THAT?!?
WAIT? OH NO! MR. INVINCIBLE?!

MR. INVINCIBLE, HELLO?! SAY SOMETHING!

OH BOY, I WAS SO SCARED! HA HA HA! I'M GLAD YOU'RE OK!

I SEE YOU! I'LL BE RIGHT THERE!
OOO... WHAT...?! OH YEAH...

SORRY, SIR! SOME CRAZY GUY WAS GONNA BLOW UP THE CITY WITH A RAY GUN!
?! WAS IT AN ANGRY LITTLE GUY WITH BLACK GLASSES?!

?!
HEH, YEAH. THAT'S THE MAD SCIENTIST! YOU DO A GREAT IMPERSONATION!

?!??
OKAY, I'LL TAKE CARE OF HIM...

NO NEED...! I ALREADY HANDLED IT!
?!

t, I TACKLED HIM JUST IN TIME TO
k HIM OFF TARGET! THEN WHACK!
SMASHED HIS DEATH MACHINE!

WOW, GREAT JOB, TOODEE! WHAT EVIL DEVICE DID HE HAVE THIS TIME?
UHH... SOME BAZOOKA THINGY TO BLOW EVERYTHING UP.

THAT'S ALL?! ARE YOU SURE?!
WELL... NOW THAT YOU MENTION IT... SOME STRANGE THINGS HAPPENED RIGHT AFTER...

31-3

31-4

Jousselin -
Colors: Croix

GREETINGS FROM THE JESTER!
A MISTER INVINCIBLE ADVENTURE
THANKS FOR COMING, MR. INVINCIBLE.
MAKE IT QUICK, JEAN-PIERRE. I PROMISED MR. DEWTILLY THAT I'D DIG HIS VEGETABLE GARDEN.
POLICE HQ

DIG HIS VEGETABLE GARDEN? WITH YOUR POWERS?
. . .
?
UHH NO, WITH A SHOVEL.

OKAY. I CALLED YOU BECAUSE THEY'RE HAVING SOME BIG PROBLEMS IN GRANDVILLE... LOOK HERE:

Daily Grandville
SPECTACULAR THEFT AT THE NATIONAL BANK
THE JESTER
A MYSTERIOUS CROOK LEAVES HIS MARK!
"Everything was gone, but there were no traces of a break-in. It's unfathomable!" Fabien Dacier Chief of Police

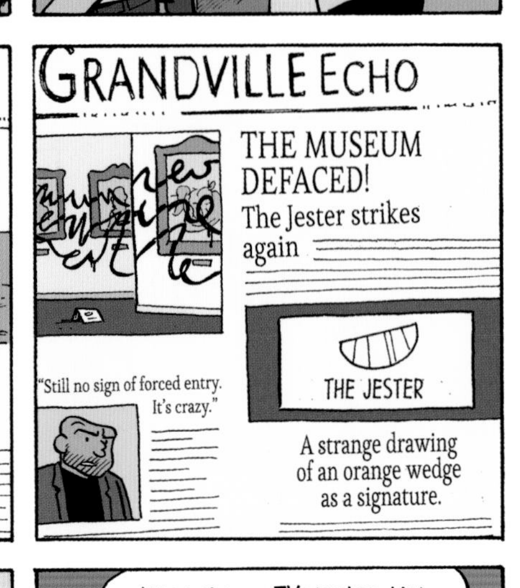
GRANDVILLE ECHO
THE MUSEUM DEFACED!
The Jester strikes again
"Still no sign of forced entry. It's crazy."
THE JESTER
A strange drawing of an orange wedge as a signature.

THE OLYMPIC POOL IS BLOWN UP!
Another attack by the now infamous Jester
"It's a miracle no one was hurt!" Fire Chief
"Everything for miles got completely soaked." Local grandma

THEFT, VANDALISM, TERRORISM... WHO COULD BE SO EVIL?
AND THAT'S NOT ALL, LOOK AT THIS...

...THIS WAS ON TV YESTERDAY...
THE JESTER: A NEW THREAT!
liveTV

MARKING HIS CRIMES WITH A DRAWING OF AN ORANGE WEDGE SHOWS AN UNDENIABLY LARGE INTELLECT. THE SYMBOLISM IS OBVIOUS: HE HAS ISSUES WITH THE FRUIT INDUSTRY...
ALEXANDER BLATTER
SPECIALIST

SURPRISE, DUMMIES!

WHAT THE...? HOW...
?!
...YOU WALKED THROUGH THE WALL!

HUH... HE WALKED THROUGH THE WALL...
NO DOY! MY POWER IS INFINITE!

Good evening, everyone. I'm the Jester.

I have the power to do whatever I want, wherever I want. You, your family, your possessions... Nobody is safe when I'm around!
Any where.

Oh boy, he's armed as well...

SO FROM NOW ON, I'M YOUR NEW MASTER, AND YOU CITIZENS OF GRANDVILLE ARE MY LOYAL SUBJECTS!
liveTV

Loyal subjects? But... er... for what reason?

You mean "for what reason, your excellency"...?
F-for what reason, y-your ex--
Because it's funny.

Speaking of which, it's time for a good laugh. I'm gonna show you the extent of my powers once again.

In 24 hours, I shall kidnap a child from this town... The mayor's son!
Go on, try to stop me.

But remember: I'm your nightmare because I'm everywhere!
Ha ha ha! Jester signing out!
liveTV

liveTV

And, uh... one more thing: my mark isn't an orange wedge. It's an evil smile, you morons!
liveTV

A madman who can walk through walls...
You see? Only you can stop this criminal, Mr. Invincible!

Can you tell Mr. Dewtilly I have to stop a madman and I'll be right back?
Yes, Mr. Invincible!

Let's not waste any time. Grandville is a few hours away. My car is parked...
No, no, I'll use my usual method. It's much simpler and a lot faster...

We'll go by telephone.
?

HELLO, GRANDVILLE TOWN HALL...
HELLO, MA'AM, PLEASE DON'T MOVE, WE'RE COMING OVER.

WHAT?
HELLO? HELLO?

HELLO?
HELLO, SIR?
ARE YOU THERE?
SIR?
PLEASE SAY SOMETHING.

PFFFFF, I HATE WEIRD CALLS LIKE THAT...
TAP
AS IF THINGS WEREN'T STRESSFUL ENOUGH WITH THIS JESTER IN TOWN...

...A HORRIBLE MAN WHO CAN JUST APPEAR OUT OF THIN AIR... TERRIFYING...

BLAM

OWW, MR. INVINCIBLE, YOU COULDA WARNED ME!
HHAAA!
?
I TOLD YOU WE'D BE COMING BY TELEPHONE...

WHO? WHAT? HANDS UP, JESTER!

THERE'S BEEN A MIX-UP, SIR. THIS IS OFFICER JEAN-PIERRE, AND MY NAME'S MISTER INVINCIBLE. WE'RE HERE TO CATCH THE JESTER, TOO.

A SMALL-TOWN COP AND A LITTLE FAT GUY IN A COSTUME... YEAH, SMELLS LIKE A TRICK TO ME.

DON'T MOVE, YOU CLOWNS!

WHAT'S GOING ON? WHO ARE THESE PEOPLE?
POLICE
UGH... THEY'RE UGLY.

STAY WHERE YOU ARE, MR. MAYOR, I THINK THESE GUYS ARE THE JESTER'S ACCOMPLICES!
OKAY, WE'VE WASTED ENOUGH TIME! LISTEN TO ME, MR. MAYOR!

THE JESTER CAN WALK THROUGH WALLS. BUT IF THERE AREN'T ANY WALLS, HE HAS NO POWER.

POLICE
There...
WRAAAAAAH!
Heh, my little Albert sure loves to shout!
POLICE

WAAOAA
Heh heh. Perfect.

Good, now that your son is safe and sound, I'm going to move on to phase two: catching the Jester!
HA HA! I'D LIKE TO SEE THAT!
WOOAAAROR

Come on, Commander, let this Mr. Invincible guy explain himself.
BUT, MR. MAYOR, HE'S WEARING A *COSTUME*! WE CAN'T TAKE SOMEONE IN A COSTUME SERIOUSLY!
ROOSHARWOHAORO

Don't be petty, Commander. It was his idea to take refuge on the roof!
Come here, you brat...
UAR

WAAAH
Not so loud, Albert. Please...

?! ALBERT!
GREETINGS FROM THE JESTER, HA HA HA!

...He walked through... the sky...
Right... things are a little trickier than I thought.
He left a note!

"If you want to see your son alive, do as I say..."
SEE?! THEY'RE HIS ACCOMPLICES! I TOLD YOU! THEY BROUGHT THE KID UP HERE ON PURPOSE!
Arrgh, shh! Let me think!

If I look at everything that just happened...
...Hmm, no. That doesn't really tell me much....

LOCK THESE TRAITORS UP!

15
5

Jousselin —
colors: Croix.

13

JOUSSELIN — COLORS: CROIX

EVEN WHEN GARDENING, HE'S...

THE ONE
AND ONLY TRUE COMIC
BOOK SUPERHERO!

JOUSSELIN – 06
COLORS: CROIX

GREETINGS FROM THE JESTER! PART TWO

HMM, NO, there's NOTHING GOIN' ON HERE...

INVINCIBLE, YOU OK?
Ooof... I THINK SO...
AH, YOU'RE AWAKE. FOLLOW ME.

SINCE YOU'RE FRIENDS WITH THE JESTER, THE MAYOR ASKED ME TO TREAT YOU NICE. BUT YOU CROOKS'LL GET WHAT'S COMING TO YA!
HUH? WE'RE NOT--

SEE? LOOK -- THE MAYOR IS DOING WHAT YOUR BOSS ASKED HIM TO DO. HAPPY NOW?!
AND SO FROM NOW ON, EVERY MORNING, WE WILL ALL BOW DOWN TO THESE GIANT PORTRAITS OF HIS MAJESTY THE JESTER...
WHAT?
IS THIS A JOKE?
SAY WHAT?!

IN THAT CASE, I'LL FREE YOUR MOUTHY LITTLE BRAT. DON'T MOVE, HE'S ON HIS WAY.
AAARGH! THE JESTER!

I SEE THAT YOU'VE DONE WHAT I ASKED. GOOD FOR YOU, YOU LITTLE TOILET MONKEYS...

AH, PERFECT...
HELLO YOU BUNCH OF MAGGOTS!

NOW THAT'S WEIRD... HE SAID EVERYTHING BACKWARDS...

MAKE WAY FOR YOUR MASTER!

NOW THAT YOU HAVE YOUR KID BACK, LET'S MOVE THINGS ALONG...
AND ONCE HE'S MOVED COMPLETELY THROUGH THE WALL, HE TALKS NORMALLY AGAIN... AHA! I'VE GOT IT!

YOU don't WANT me to start USING MY powers for evil AGAIN, do YOU? ALRIGHT, then... YOU'RE GONNA...
Hold on, let me think...

Now that he's brought the kid back, you can go beat him up, right?
I think I finally understand how the Jester's powers work!

HMM... WHAT SHOULD I ASK FOR NOW? Let me see... SOMETHING THAT'LL REALLY ANNOY ALL OF YOU...
HA! I KNOW!

I HEREBY BAN ALL CONSUMPTION OF POTATOES IN GRANDVILLE. CHIPS, FRIES, HASH BROWNS, MASHED... NO MORE! BANNED!

THAT'S GONNA BE ANNOYING, RIGHT? EVERYONE LOVES POTATOES, RIGHT?!
OKAY, NOW, BOW DOWN BEFORE YOUR MASTER.

Master Jester... dare I ask for an exclusive interview?
Yeah sure, no problem, trashbag. My people will be in touch.

NOW I WISH YOU ALL A TERRIBLE, SWEATY DAY! HA HA HA! JESTER... OUT!

OKAY. Got it.

LISTEN UP, EVERYONE. MY NAME IS MISTER INVINCIBLE AND I'M GOING TO CAPTURE THE JESTER. SO, YOU CAN STOP ACTING LIKE A BUNCH OF COWARDS!

WHAT?! HEY! WE'RE NOT COWARDS!
AND POTATOES ARE GROSS!
HIS MAJESTY THE JESTER IS A GREAT MAN!
YEAH! DOWN WITH POTATOES!

HIS MAJESTY'S ENEMIES ARE NOT WELCOME IN GRANDVILLE!
YEAH! GET OUT!
DIRTY POTATO MUNCHERS!
Er... let's go before things turn ugly...
16
3

WHAT NOW, MR. INVINCIBLE?
NOW? I'M GOING TO ARREST THE JESTER!
WE CAN'T LET THAT LOON RUN AMOK, CAN WE?

A SKILLET? VERY GOOD, SIR.
ANYTHING ELSE? ALL POTATO FRYERS ARE NOW 50% OFF...
BIG BAZAR

UM... WHAT'S THAT FOR, MR. INVINCIBLE?
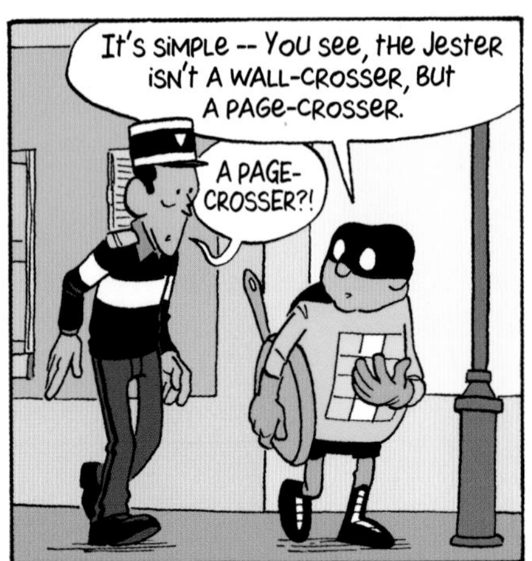
IT'S SIMPLE -- YOU SEE, THE JESTER ISN'T A WALL-CROSSER, BUT A PAGE-CROSSER.
A PAGE-CROSSER?!

YEP, AND HE CROSSED PAGES RIGHT IN THE MIDDLE OF STRIP 3 IN HIS ESCAPE EARLIER...
THE MIDDLE OF WHAT?!

...WHICH MEANS THAT HE'LL REAPPEAR RIGHT ABOUT...

...NOW.
BONG

THE JESTER!
HA HA! MISTER INVINCIBLE, YOU'RE THE BEST!

NO WAY! I WAS TAILING YOU GUYS, CONVINCED THAT YOU'D LEAD ME TO THE JESTER'S SECRET LAIR, AND... HAH!

US "CROOKS" SAVED THE TOWN...
UH... YEAH... I OWE YOU AN APOLOGY...
POLICE

NOW HOW DO WE KEEP A WALL-CROSSER LOCKED UP...?
A PAGE-CROSSER YOU MEAN!
YOU CAN STOP DUMPING THOSE FRIES NOW, SIR.
16
4

Jousselin – colors: Croix

16
5

Around 12 of them... they've organized a sit-in on my property.

A bunch of pacifists... yes, two police vans should be enough to hold them all.
PESTICHEM PLANET KILLERS!
PESTICHEM = POLLUTERS
STOP!
SHAME ON YOU!

C'mon, everyone, all together, for Madam CEO...
WE'VE ONLY GOT ONE PLAA-NET!

DON'T TAKE IT FOR GRAAN-TED!
Oh no, please, Mom, not the song...

We've only got one plaa-net!
Oh boy, embarrassing...
TOODEE'S VACATION
A MISTER INVINCIBLE ADVENTURE

Hey, Mr. Invincible? It's Two-Dee boy.
Hey, Toodee. How's your trip?

Well... I told you that my mom was taking me to a little island, right? Uh, well, we came here because the CEO of pesti-whatever has a house on the island. You know, that chemical company....?

Now my mom and her friends are singing in the CEO's yard to try to convince them to stop polluting...

So I'm out here on my own, in my costume, looking for superhero stuff to do. But, pfff... there's nothing.

HUH?! WHAT THE...?!

OH NOOOO...
WHAT? WHAT IS IT?
I... ACCIDENTALLY KNOCKED A BABY BIRD FROM ITS NEST... AND NOW IT'S HUGE!

YEESH. YOU SHOULD GET IT BACK BEFORE IT TRASHES THE PLACE.
BUT IT'S JUST A BABY! I'M SCARED I'LL HURT IT! I MIGHT END UP SQUISHING IT WITH MY SUPER POWERS INSTEAD OF CATCHING IT. I'M FREAKING OUT!

WE'VE ONLY GOT ONE PLAA-NET!
POLICE
POLICE
STOP!

DON'T TAKE IT FOR GRAAN-TED!
ENJOY THE SLAMMER, DO-GOODERS!

PFFF... BUNCH OF CLOWNS... WHAT ARE THEY HOPING TO ACHIEVE WITH THAT PATHETIC SONG?

IF OUR "PESTICHEM" PRODUCTS WERE THAT HARMFUL, MOTHER NATURE WOULD SEND SOME LITTLE RABBITS AND BIRDS TO TELL ME TO STOP! HA HA HA!

TOODEE, YOU REALLY NEED TO HURRY... THINGS ARE TURNING NASTY...
I KNOW, I KNOW! I'M LOOKING FOR A WAY TO GET THE BIRD BACK HERE...!

OKAY! I... I KNOW THAT OUR PRODUCTS ARE SERIOUSLY BAD FOR NATURE... BUT IT... IT ISN'T BECAUSE I'M A NASTY PERSON... I JUST DO IT FOR THE MONEY, YOU KNOW?

Jousselin —
colors: Croix.

OFF-SEASON TRAVEL

AAAH! WHAT THE HECK...?!
UM... A LITTLE SNAFU. NO NEED TO PANIC.
?!?

I-I'LL CALL FOR HELP!
NO, NO! I'LL TAKE IT BACK TO ITS NATURAL HABITAT! GET THE BOOK! READ THE PARAGRAPH AGAIN!

OK OK...
QUICK!
THERE... MR. INVINCIBLE?
?!

TheArcticissituatedintheNorth
Poleitscenterisavasteternally
frozenseaArcticcomesfrom
arktosAncientGreekforbear
areferencetotheconstellation

UrsaMajortheGreatBearan
amusing coincidencepolar
bearsareonlyfoundinthe
ArcticandnotintheAntarctic.

READ IT AGAIN, JEAN-PIERRE! BUT SLOWER! MUCH SLOWER!

OK... UM...
The Arrrctic is situuuated...

...in the Nooooorth Pooole.
?
OKAY, NOW--
!!

Its centeeeer isss aaa...
AHHHH! THE BOTTOM OF THE PAGE!

24-2

JOUSSELIN-
COLORS: CROIX.

JOUSSELIN -
COUL.: CROIX

33

JOUSSELIN-
COUL. : CROIX.

THE ONE AND ONLY TRUE COMIC BOOK SUPERHERO!

IN

RETURN OF THE JESTER!

Just three more minutes...

HRM.

Detective Dacier here...
No, it's fine, I'm stopped by some roadwork. What's up?

Yeah, my wife and kids are fine. Yeah, mom, too...
BINGO!
?!

Yeah, sure, the weather's great...
WHY ARE YOU CALLING ME?!

WHAT?!

A pick axe?! Where'd he get a pick axe?!

But we installed cameras to keep an eye on him!

Maybe we shoulda bought you new glasses, too!
HA HA! Freedom!

GOOD JOB, YOU iDiOTS! Hope you're proud of yourselves!

Later, suckers!
RRRRGH! NO WAY!

Who assigned those losers?!

It's 15 to 6! You ready?
Hang on...

Hello?
Oh, Hi, Detective!

Mr. Invincible, Bad news: The Jester escaped!
POLICE

Ah.
I see.

We need your help! Only you can stop him!
POLICE

Okay, I'll take care of it... But we can't see him now. I'll have to wait for the next page spread.

Huh? The next what?
Wait, don't hang up...! Hello? HELLO?!
POLICE

You ready?

?

Alright, let's go!
Okay... serving!

Wait?! The Jester could strike at any minute! Has Mr. Invincible lost his mind?!
LICE

No, I haven't lost my mind. Trust me!
AAAH! WHAT...?!

Detective, the men are ready. What are our orders?
Uh...
...we trust Mr. Invincible and wait...

25-3

Mr. Invincible!
Hey, JP!

I came as soon as I got your message.
Thanks! I need your help. The Jester escaped.

You... need me?! But, uh... sure! You can count on me!
Great.

?

Are we... waiting for something?
Yeah for the next page, so I can...
Oops. Too late.

Take a look...
Perfect! He's over there...
...oh, haha! That's a good one!
?

It's fine. The Jester will stop himself.
?

We just need a way to get him before he wakes up...
Hmm...
?

Hey, would you mind giving me a push?
?

Uh... what do I do about the Jester...?
Nothing, JP! I'll take care of it!

Just keep an eye on my nephew while I'm gone.
Okay, here I go...!

Your nephew. Sure.

AH HAHA! It feels Good to HAVE MY evil toys BACK!
Get ReAdy, GRANdVILLe! YOUR WORST NIGHTMARe is BACK!

I cooked something to celebrate, Boss! Tell me what you think...

Did you find out anything about that little yellow gnome that sent me to prison?
OH, YeAH!

He's CALLed MR. INVINCIBLE And He's some kindA wizard. He CAN do ALL kinds of things no one understands...
It's kindA creepy...

MAGIC, HUH...? THAT explains how he got me last time...

He really just caught me by surprise, the buffoon...

...But he won't get me twice! I'M ON GUARD NOW! HA HA HA!

?!
?!

MR. INVINCIBLE?! Is this one of your magic tricks?!
HUH? No wait! We already--

Nice try, Bozo! I'M MUCH SMARTER THAN THAT!

If he found my hideout, I better get outta here...

Woop! Sorry!

HMM... WHAT CAN I tie him up with...?
Try some of this, Boss! It's duck soup!

AAAHH! THE WIZARD!
?

Please don't hurt me! Have mercy!
UH, OKAY. But give me that apron...

25.5

25-6

Jousselin -
coul. : Croix

THE ONE AND ONLY TRUE COMIC BOOK SUPERHERO!

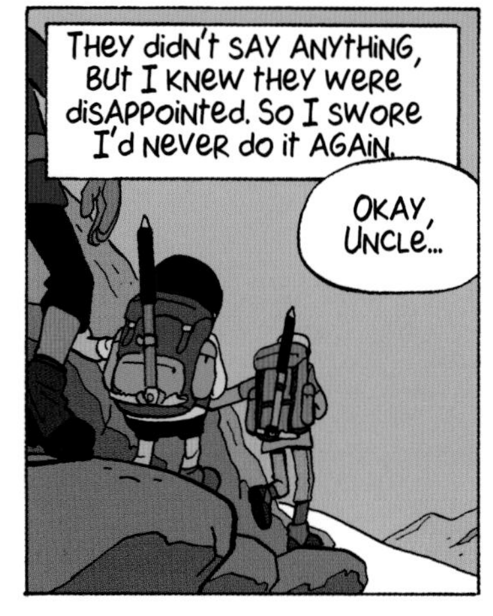

JOUSSELIN -
COUL. : CROIX

THE MYSTERIOUS LADY
A MISTER INVINCIBLE ADVENTURE

PFFF NOTHING'S HAPPENING!
YEAH, IT'S NICE, HUH?

BORED, BORED, BORED...

?!

?!
HER SANDWICH...

?!

SHE'S WALKING... BACKWARD?!
THAT MEANS...

Nice dAY, HUH?
WHOA! WHY'Re YOU SO ANGRY? I don't WANt tRouBLe...

HUH?! ANGRY? I WAS Just tRYiNG to Be Polite!
?!

Yep, No doUBt ABOUt it...
...tHAt WOMAN is LiViNG BACKWARds!

OoPS!
SORRY!

CAN I HAVe MY BALL BACK...
?!
YouR WHAt?

? But... WHeRe'd YOU...

AH, theRe!

HMM, THIS IS COMPLEX...
So EVERYTHING SHE does HAPPENS IN REVERSE ORDER...

WOW, to BE GOING IN THE OPPOSITE direction FROM EVERYONE MUST GET TIRING...

OH, NO! HER PACK!

I CAN FIX THIS...

OOOF!

?
EXCUSE ME, MISS...

WHA... HOW...?
YOU dropped YOUR BACKPACK. YOU MIGHT WANT to FIX it...

? HUH?
I, UH... don't WORRY! It WILL ALL WORK OUT...

I'LL NEED SOME NEW CLOTHES, A NEW SLEEPING BAG...
...AS IF LIVING BACKWARDS WASN'T HARD ENOUGH!

THAT BAG HAD ALL MY THINGS IN IT... NOW ITS GONE!

39.4

JOUSSELIN – COUL. : CROIX

ON MY WAY!
I'LL GRAB SOME BREAD...
ALTERNATE CHAOS
A MISTER INVINCIBLE ADVENTURE

?
HA HA! FINISHED!

WHAT'S GOING ON, YOU MAD MAN?!
?! I'M NOT MAD!

DOES THIS LOOK LIKE THE WORK OF A MAD MAN?
WELL... ACTUALLY...

THIS IS MY ALTERNATE REALITY MACHINE! AND IT WILL BRING YOUR ULTIMATE DEMISE! HA HA HA!

Y'KNOW, ALL OF THOSE ELECTRICAL CABLES ON THE SIDEWALK IS DANGEROUS, ESPECIALLY IN THIS RAIN...
WELL, YEAH, BUT MY MACHINE NEEDS LOTS OF ELECTRICITY...

...DON'T CHANGE THE SUBJECT! I WAS TELLING YOU ABOUT MY DIABOLICAL PLAN!

ONE PULL OF THIS LEVER AND BOOM! THIS MACHINE WILL SPLIT OUR UNIVERSE INTO TWO SEPARATE REALITIES!
A
B

OKAY, BUT WHY?
WHY? IF THERE'S AN ALTERNATE REALITY, I CAN AVOID YOU!

EVEN IF THIS THINGY WORKS, WE'LL STILL END UP FIGHTING EACH OTHER...
WH... NO! LOOK, IF IN REALITY A I DO ONE THING AND IN REALITY B I DO ANOTHER... THEN I CAN... UM...

...OKAY SO I HAVEN'T WORKED OUT EVERY DETAIL OF MY PLAN YET, BUT WHEN I DO, YOU'LL --
?
KLIK!

VRRRR
WHAT?! BLASTED BIRD! YOU TURNED IT ON!

I BETTER TURN IT OFF BEFORE IT'S TOO LATE!
THAT THING DOESN'T LOOK VERY SAFE...!

CLOUC
I'LL TURN IT BACK ON WHEN I HAVE A PLAN...
THAT WON'T MATTER...

CLOUC
CLOUC
CLOUC
BUT... NO...
IT'S NOT TURNING OFF! IT'S OVERHEATING!

ARGH! STUPID MACHINE!
LOOK OUT!

ATTACKING ME FROM BEHIND?! A CHEAP MOVE, HERO!
VRRR
...!

MY MACHINE MIGHT NOT WORK, BUT I CAN STILL GET YOU WITH ELECTRICITY! HA!
OH BOY...

YEEOW!

ARE YOU DONE WITH THIS NONSENSE?
...

KLOK
GOOD.
SIGH

'S NOT A STOPLIGHT! THIS SOME KINDA JOKE?!
GAH! BETTER TURN IT OFF BEFORE...

Y'KNOW, IF YOU'D BEEN WEARING A SEATBELT...
?

STAY OUTTA THIS, WEIRDO.
BONK

POF!

SIGH ANOTHER HUMILIATING DEFEAT.
TRIED TO WARN
, BUT YOU NEVER LISTEN...

AREN'T YOU TIRED OF DOING STUPID THINGS? ANNOYING PEOPLE ALL THE TIME?
IT REALLY GETS TIRESOME...

FINE.
SIGH
KLOK

DOUSSELIN –
COUL. : CROIX

SOME SAY THEY'VE SEEN HIM FLY!

THE ONE AND ONLY TRUE COMIC BOOK SUPERHERO!

JOUSSELIN –
COULEURS : CROIX

THE ONE AND ONLY TRUE COMIC BOOK SUPERHERO!

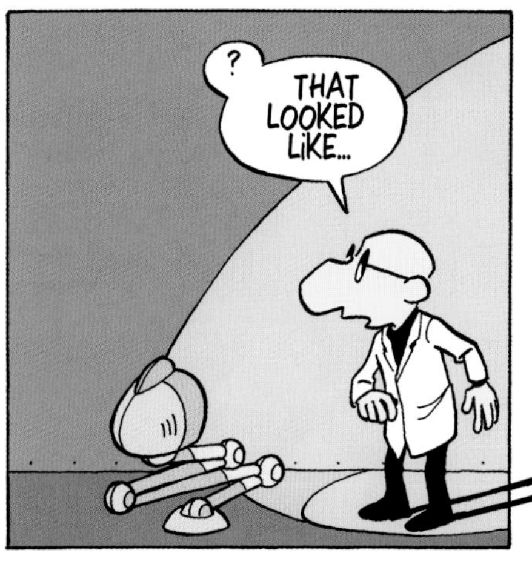

(*)

JOUSSELIN - COUL. : CROIX

...SO WE CUT THEM BACK EVERY YEAR BEFORE THE BUDS COME OUT...
AMERICAN EXPRESS
A MISTER INVINCIBLE ADVENTURE

HEY, IT'S JEAN-PIERRE...
RIGHT HERE! STOP! PLEASE! STOP!

MRS. SIGOURNEY HERE HAS BEEN LOOKING FOR YOU...
MR. INVINCIBLE! WHY, IT'S SUCH A PLEASURE TO MEET YOU!

I'VE HEARD ABOUT YOUR EXTRAORDINARY DEEDS WHILE HERE ON VACATION, AND I THINK YOU MIGHT BE ABLE TO SOLVE MY PROBLEM...!

YOU SEE, MY GRANDSON COULD USE YOUR HELP!
NO PROBLEM!

WHERE IS HE?
UH, WELL, THERE'S JUST ONE THING...

...MY COUNTRY'S ARMED FORCES HAVE FAILED AT THIS, AND IF ONE LITTLE MAN WERE TO SOLVE IT... IT COULD BE EMBARASSING. IT MIGHT LOOK BETTER IF YOU BROUGHT OTHER HEROS WITH YOU...

"YOUR COUNTRY'S ARMED FORCES"...? WHAT'S THIS ALL ABOUT?

I'M SORRY, I HAVEN'T EXPLAINED THINGS VERY WELL...
SEE, MY COUNTRY IS UNDER ATTACK BY AN ADVERSARY THAT OUR ARMED FORCES AND SUPERHEROES HAVEN'T BEEN ABLE TO STOP...
I ONLY KNOW ABOUT THIS BECAUSE MY GRANDSON IS THE PRESIDENT OF THE UNITED STATES OF AMERICA.

...
THE WHO NOW...?
OKAY, WELL, LET'S GATHER A TEAM AND GO!
BUT LET'S HURRY... MY NEPHEW'S SCHOOL PLAY IS TONIGHT...

Here's TooDee!
Between him, JP, Mr. Jack, and myself, will that be enough?
That would be perfect! You're so considerate!
I'll call my grandson to let him know!

Then we can use the call to get there. Okay, everyone...
What can I do?
...gather around.
Don't forget: old man Jack's power only works when he's annoyed!

Hello? It's Grandma...
Hi, Gramy. What's up?
Everyone holding on...?
Where to?

I'm on my way with a bunch of local superheroes to help!
Er, thanks, Mom, but we're in a bit over our heads here...
Jump!

That was my grandma. She's sending some superheroes to help us out...
tip
What?!

Mr. President, we can handle this monster! Besides... this situation is supposed to be a *top secret national security issue!*

C'mon, General Beefsteak. They're friendly. And you know we're running out of options...

Ah! The Band of Warriors has arrived! Perfect timing!

Hey, Gramy.
How'd you get in here?!
What'd he say?
Oh, right... does anyone speak American?
I'm learning some in school... I'm getting a C-!

Argh, I can't understand a word they're saying...
It's okay, General. I know a little...
Hello! Welcome!
Thanks!
It's an honor...
Who's that? Where are we?

SERIOUSLY... WHERE...?!
PLEASE, FOLLOW ME.

WAIT... ARE WE IN AMERICA?!
YOU DON'T LOOK SO GOOD... ARE YOU EATING ENOUGH FRUIT?
THE ENEMY IS VERY STRONG. HE HAS DESTROYED A LOT...

WHOA! THAT'S CRICKET BOY! I'M A HUGE FAN!
ARE THE BANDAGES PART OF HIS COSTUME?

MY EYES! MY POOR EYES!
SHHH... THERE, THERE. IT'S OVER. YOU'RE SAFE NOW...
THE PIPISTRELLE! THE GREATEST HERO EVER! WHAT...

...RAPIDUS THE LIGHTNING GUY?!
THESE HEROES HAVE COME TO HELP US. THEY'RE FROM... EUROPE.

DON'T GO OUT THERE! RUN! BEFORE IT'S TOO LATE!
WHAT'S HE SAYING?
I DUNNO, BUT IT'S NOT EXACTLY REASSURING...

UH... MR. INVINCIBLE? THEY'RE ALL PRETTY BEAT UP... ARE WE SURE WE...
IT'LL BE FINE, TOODEÉ.

All these soldiers look exhausted...
Hmm, yeah...
That's the Adversary's magic...

He's stopped the sun from setting!
We haven't seen night in a week! Constant daylight. Ruining everyone's sleep...

Someone who can stop time locally...?
I don't like that...
And I don't like all these weapons everywhere...

So where are we headed, sir?
Over there. The Adversary has taken over part of the city. Made a barricade.

What the heck is that?!

Alright, time to go to work, friends!

WAIT! I'M GOING WITH THEM!

UM, HEY, MR. INVINCIBLE? SINCE WE DON'T REALLY KNOW WHAT THAT THING IS, SHOULDN'T WE MAYBE USE OLD MAN JACK'S SUPERPOWER...?
YEAH, GOOD IDEA!
WHAT ARE THEY SAYING...? ARE THEY PLOTTING SOMETHING?!

SURE, IF YOU WANT.
DON'T FORGET -- HE NEEDS TO BE ANNOYED TO USE HIS POWER...

UH...
...HEY, YOU OLD COOT!

I MEAN... SORRY. I DIDN'T...
YEAH, I GET IT.

HEY, I AGREE WITH YOU -- BOCCE BALL REALLY IS A GAME FOR DUMMIES...
C'MON. YOU'RE TRYING TOO HARD.

KICK!

I-I WAS JUST TRYIN' TO MAKE YOU MAD...
OKAY, NOTHING'S WORKING, SO LET'S MOVE ON!
HOLY ROCKETS, WHAT'S WITH THIS BAND OF WACKOS?

TAP TAP

IT'S OKAY! IT'S SOLID! WE CAN WALK ON IT!

Oof!

I think there's a car here...
BONK!

And a lamp post here...
And a trashcan here...

This is still the city... but everything is totally black!
Okay, let's try to stay in the middle of the road so we don't bump into things...

Which way do we go? This darkness is gigantic!
Let's just keep going and hope we find something...
That'll take too long! I have to be at the school tonight!

Wait, I have an idea...

When you can't see the bottom of a well, you throw a stone in it to hear the "plop"...

There! Something that's not black!
Good job, Toodee!

UNBELIEVABLE!
Let's Go!

?!
SWIIP
?!
?!
ROULROUL
DZOIING

Empty bottles?
Stretched string...
A BANANA peel...

The street's BOOBY trapped!
We must Be getting close to something important...

...But with all these traps, it'll take forever to get to the hole Toodee made...
...

Stand back and wait for me...!

OKAY, don't move!

There! I made a path for us!

THAT KID WOULD MAKE ONE HECK OF A WEAPON...
Well done!

Ah, yeah... much better without BANANA peels...

Everything's normal...
Except the sky...

Stores, a park... someone made a nice little hideout here...

Alright, CHROMALINE! We found your hideout! HA HA HA!
?
?

C'mon out, Chromaline! Show yourself! Stop hiding!
What's up?
I can't understand what he's saying, but I don't like the way he's waving that gun around!

?!

YAAAH!
Pow! Pow!
?

Hmm...

I prefer to talk when your gun is empty, General...
A kid?
38/08

WHAT DO I HAVE TO DO TO MAKE YOU UNDERSTAND?!

WHEN ARE YOU ALL GOING TO JUST LEAVE ME ALONE?!
?!!

AGH! MY EYES!
The COLORS ARE VIBRATING...!
HUH? WHAT'S WRONG, GUYS?

HUH?! We CAN't see!
?!
I see some strange shapes and shades, but... ...oh, I get it!

MY SCHOOL NURSE told Me I WAS COLOR BLIND! THAT MUST Be it!
You're supposed to see NUMBERS in the COLORS But I COULDN'T... HeH...

Then it's up to you to stop her, Toodee!
But... she's A GIRL! I CAN't hit A GIRL!

UM... eXCUSE Me...
...YOU SPEAK FRENCH?

STAY BACK!

WHOA...

SHE CONTROLS COLORS!

38/09

WH... WHO IS SHE?!
WHAT did SHE SAY to the GENERAL?
...I dUNNO...

YOU don't KNOW?! YOU SAid YOU SPOKE AMERICAN! WERE YOU LYING?!
NO, tHEY JUSt tALK fASt! ANd tHEIR ACCENt...
?

Ooo, if tHERE'S ONE tHING I REALLY HAtE it'S LiARS!
...But, But, I...
SSHH! Let HIM Get ANGRY! It'LL ACtiVAtE HIS POWER!

And YOU WItH YOUR GUNS...!
CHKRONG!
?!
WHAt do YOU NEEd tHOSE tHINGS FOR?!

?!
Y'KNOW, WORdS ARE MORE POWERFUL tHAN ANY WEAPON IN tHE WORLd!
BONK
BONK
BONK

He'S RUNNiNG!
ALONE ANd UNARMEd... NOt A GREAt SOLdiER...

WELL, WE MAY BE BEttER OFF ON OUR OWN... WE NEEd tO tALK tO tHAt GiRL ANd FINd OUt WHAt'S GOiNG ON.
WHAt if SHE tRiES tO BLINd US AGAIN BEFORE WE CAN SAY ANYtHiNG?

HMM, I MAY HAVE AN idEA... tHIS WAY!
HAPPY TIME

101
HAPPY TIME
101

HAH! PARtY'S OVER! Let'S SEE HER tRY tO BLINd US NOW!
WOOOUUHH...
TIME
?
I HEAR A dOG...

OVER tHERE...
WOOOUUHH

SSHH! Quiet, Spike! It's just me, CHROMALINE!
I KNOW YOU don't like WHEN I do the CHAMELEON thing, BUT I HAd to Get AWAY from the GeneRAL...

I'M SUCH A dUMMY... If I HAdN't used my powers At tHAT student party, no one would have known I HAd them...
I think she's French!

...And tHAT jerk General wouldn't be trying to capture me...
What Are we gonna do, Spike?
She seems nice!

Uh... hello...
?! You again!
Listen, miss... we're from France, And...
...And you want me to work for you, too?!

NEVER! Do you hear me? I'll never use my powers as a military weapon!
Huh? That's not what we...

You've got it wrong, miss...
It's... not working!

Don't come any closer!
They're weaing sunglasses! I have to figure something else out... fast!

Please, just listen for a minute...
!

There's no point making everything the same color... your black zone didn't stop us from...
?!
...

Hey... that's not funny...

WAIT! WE'RE ON YOUR SIDE!

Oh, man...
DARN.

WHAT do we do NOW, MR. INVINCIBLE?

DON'T PANIC. WE'LL JUST MAKE A CALL AND JUMP TO THAT NEW LOCATION.
THEN I'LL FIND A WAY TO FIX THIS.

SO, UM... does ANYONE HAVE AN INTERNATIONAL PLAN ON THEIR PHONE?

...
A WHAT?

OY.
SO I GUESS THAT MEANS NONE OF OUR PHONES WORK HERE.

And if we try to feel our way out of here, it'll take forever!
LOOK! A PIGEON!

OH YEAH!
He must've come from the outside! There aren't any obstacles in the sky...
WHAT if we try to fly out of here...?

I CAN do A lot of things, but flying isn't one them...
I CAN use the power of words to fly...
?!

WH-WHAT'S HAPPENING?!
?!
?!
...BUT to do it, I've gotta talk non-stop, so it's easier if I sing...

WHOA...
I'll be where the eagles fly... higher and higher...!
Good job, JACK!
38/12

Yes! We're out of the ORANGE!
I'LL Be YOUR MAN IN Motion... I JUST GottA SiiiNNNNG...!

But NOW we're in the pitch BLACK SKY... we CAN't see A thiNG!
No CHoice... keep GoiNG...
CAReful, MR. JACK...
TAKe me where the LiGht is BRiGHteR AND BRiiiiGHteRRR...

...I thiiiNK I foRRGot the WoRRRds...
WeLL, if we're tRYiNG to Be SNeAKY, too LAte...

YeSSS!
We MAde it BACK to the City!
I'LL Be where the eAGLeS fLY... HiGHeR AND HiGHeR...!

There's the ARMY HQ!
HMM, A Lot of ACtioN dowN theRe...
I'M GettiNG A soRe THROOOAt fRoM SiiiNGiNG...

LOOK! They're MOViNG iN!
HAAANG ONNN...
They're usiNG Toodee's PATH to iNVAde CHROMALiNe's Hideout!

?
?
?
I'LL Be the eAGLe LANdiNG LoweR AND LoweRRRR... No MoRe MAN iN MotioN...

WHAt's GoiNG oN? WHY ARe We fALLiNG?!
If we HAd wheeLS, we CoULd LAAANd... iNsteAd we're GoNNA CRAAAASH...

EVERYONE OKAY?
YEAH... SORTA...

?
WOUUHH!
?

!
!

IT'S CHROMALINE!
SHE'S HERE! THE GIRL'S HERE!

LOOKS LIKE SOMETHING'S GOING ON OVER THERE...
I SEE IT...

...AND THAT'S ENOUGH VIOLENCE FOR TODAY!

THERE!
YOU CAN'T DO YOUR COLOR THING IF YOU CAN'T SEE!

NOW LISTEN UP, YOUNG LADY! I'M NOT YOUR ENEMY! WE'RE HERE TO HELP YOU!

WHAT'S THAT ORANGE BLOB?
?
IT'S THAT FAT FRENCH HERO! HAH!
HOO-RAH!
WE GOT HER!

BRAVO, MR. INVINCIBLE! YOU CAPTURED THE ENEMY! THANK YOU!

38/45

Joussellin - Croix.

WATCH OUT, CHIEF! MUD PUDDLE TO YOUR RIGHT...

BONK
OOP. SORRY, CHIEF.
WE MADE IT!
YOU CAN TAKE OFF THE BLINDFOLD, CAPTAIN!

HAPPY BIRTHDAY!
THE GREAT BEYOND
A MISTER INVINCIBLE ADVENTURE
WHOA! A SURPRISE PICNIC!

FOR YOU, CHIEF!
A GALAXY QUEST D-2399 TELESCOPE! THEY SAY IT'S THE BEST!
WOW, THAT'S SO NICE...! THANKS!

I DIDN'T KNOW YOU LIKE ASTRONOMY, JP!
I, UH... DIDN'T EITHER!
HUH?

BUT YOU SAID...
NO, NO, LEONARD SAID...
BUT I THOUGHT SHE SAID...
GUYS! THIS IS GREAT!

IT'S A CHANCE TO LEARN NEW THINGS!
ABOUT PLANETS AND STUFF!

AND LOOK! I NEVER KNEW THAT SHOOTING STARS COULD BE GREEN...! WOW!

?
A GREEN SHOOTING STAR?
WHAT THE...
IT'S HEADED RIGHT AT US!
36-1

EVERYONE OKAY?
WHEW! A FEW FEET OVER AND THAT METEORITE WOULDA HIT THE CAKE!

HMM... THAT'S NOT A METEORITE...

?!

?!

WHATAYA KNOW...

A MARTIAN?!
HE COPIED YOU, MR. INVINCIBLE!
HUH? I'M NOT THAT... ROUND... AM I?
?!
?!
?!

WOW! HE COPIED MY SUPERPOWERS, TOO!

UM... WELCOME, TRAVELER!
THE COOLER!

AW, MAN! THAT HAD ALL OF OUR DRINKS IN IT!
IT'S OKAY... I KNOW HOW THIS WORKS! THE COOLER WILL SHOW UP IN THE FUTURE, RIGHT?
UH... NO.

IT FELL INTO THE GREAT BEYOND. IT'S GONE FOREVER.
?
?
36-2

The Great Beyond?!
Yeah, infinite emptiness.
But let's welcome our visitor!

Greetings, friend from another world! On behalf of the planet Earth, welcome!
I'm Jean--

POW

He didn't come in peace! He didn't come in peace!

Mr. Invincible... wake uuup!

Huh...?
Whew! It's gone crazy!

Wh-what's going on...?!
He almost knocked you into the Great Beyond...!

LOOK OUT!

EVERYONE HOLD ONTO SOMETHING STURDY! HURRY!

WHY ARE YOU ATTACKING US, TRAVELER?

YOU'RE STARTING TO GET ON MY NERVES...

TELL US WHAT YOU WANT!
WHY ARE YOU RUNNING AROUND?
WHO CARES?!

HE'S A KILLER MARTIAN!
KNOCK 'IM OUT! HURRY!
BEFORE HE KNOCKS YOU INTO THE GREAT BEYOND!

I'd prefer to KNOW YOUR intentions, traveler... But you've Left me no choice. I'M GONNA HAVE to Hit YOU.
Get HIM, MR. INVINCIBLE!

?!

MR. INVINCIBLE?!
He fell into the Great Beyond...

N-NO, JUST WAIT... HE'LL BE BACK...

...He's invincibile...
YeAH, But the MARTIAN copied His power... so He is, too!

Nooo... it's not possible... Mr. Invincible...

MR. INVINCIBLE!
WOOHOO! YOU'RE ALIVE!
WHAT'S WRONG?

HE PUNCHED THE CAKE AND IT MADE HIM CRAZY!
IT'S LIKE HE DOESN'T UNDERSTAND WHAT IT IS... LIKE HE'S NEVER SEEN ANYTHING LIKE IT!
SQUISHY THINGS! HIT HIM WITH SQUISHY THINGS!

"NEVER SEEN ANYTHING LIKE IT..." BINGO! THAT'S IT!
HE'S FROM A COMPLETELY DIFFERENT WORLD... EVERYTHING HERE MUST SEEM STRANGE AND TERRIFYING!

IT'S MAKING HIM PANIC! THAT'S WHY HE'S ACTING CRAZY!
HE DOESN'T WANT TO HURT US, HE'S JUST TERRIFIED!

I HAVE TO FIND A WAY TO SEND HIM BACK TO HIS WORLD...

?
POC

HMM... YEAH, THAT COULD WORK...

YOU'RE GONNA GIVE HIM CHAMPAGNE?! WON'T THAT MAKE THINGS WORSE?!

?!

UH OH...

36-6

JOUSSELIN –
COUL. : CROIX.

HE CAN PROVE SCIENTIFIC THEORIES!

BUT... WEREN'T YOU LISTENING?!
YOU'RE IM-MOB-IL-IZED! YOU CAN'T MOVE! HAHAHA!

YEAH, BUT MY FUTURE SELF WILL FREE ME.
?! YOUR FUTURE SELF IS CAUGHT, TOO! HE CAN'T HELP YOU!

SURE HE CAN. BECAUSE I'LL BE FREE IN A MINUTE.
?! HUH?

OH, I GET IT... YOU'RE TRYING TO TRICK ME! HA HA!
WELL, IT WON'T WORK!

AAAH!
BOY, HE SURE IS ANNOYING...

N... NO! THAT'S IMPOSSIBLE... HOW...
OKAY, I'LL EXPLAIN IT AGAIN...

BECAUSE I CAME TO FREE MYSELF, I AM ABLE TO COME FREE MYSELF.
IT'S CALLED A PARADOX.

I'M INVINCIBLE. SOME DAY YOU'LL GET IT.

BUT... HE'S JUST LEAVING ME?

WHEW! TIME TO RUN!

"BECAUSE I CAME TO FREE MYSELF, I AM ABLE TO COME FREE MYSELF."
?! THAT MAKES NO SENSE!

HIII!
NOT SO FAST!

FIRST, YOU'RE GONNA APOLOGIZE.
THEN YOU'RE GONNA FIX THINGS.

AUSE I CAME TO FREE
M ABLE TO COME FREE
CAUSE I CAME TO FREE
AM ABLE TO COME FREE M
CAUSE I CAME TO FREE
ABLE TO COME FREE
Y'KNOW, CHALLENGING MR. INVINCIBLE IS NEVER A GOOD IDEA. DON'T THEY TEACH KIDS TO THINK ANYMORE THESE DAYS?
28-2
JOUSSELIN - COUL.: CROIX.